THIS BLOOMSBURY BOOK

BELONGS TO

Ciara

For Inigo – L.B.
For Grandma and Grandad – R.B.

First published in Great Britain in 1999 by Bloomsbury Publishing Plc
38 Soho Square, London W1V 5DF
This paperback edition first published in 2000

A CIP catalogue record for this book is available from the British Library.
ISBN 0 7475 4674 6 (paperback)
ISBN 0 7475 4122 1 (hardback)

Designed by Dawn Apperley
Printed by South China Printing Co.in Hong Kong

1 3 5 7 9 10 8 6 4 2

Fran's Flower

Lisa Bruce and Rosalind Beardshaw

BLOOMSBURY
CHILDREN'S
BOOKS

One day Fran found a flowerpot filled with soil. Poking out of the top was a tiny tip. "I will grow this flower," Fran said to Fred.

She took it home.
"Grow flower," she said.
But the tip stayed tiny.

Go on, grow!

"I think the flower is hungry," Fran told Fred.

Of course it is

So Fran went to the fridge.
She found some of her favourite food.

She gave the flower a slice of pizza.

Uh oh!

The next day Fran gave it a piece of cheeseburger.

She gave it spaghetti, two chocolate biscuits and a large spoonful of strawberry ice-cream.

Good grief!

She even gave it one of Fred's juicy bones.

But the flower didn't grow. The tip stayed tiny.
Fran got fed up.

There she goes

"Silly flower," she said, and she threw it out of the back door.

Rain, rain
go away!

The flowerpot fell on the ground and rolled
away. The rain fell on it.

The wind blew on it.

I wish

The sun shone on it.

It grew ...

and grew ...

and grew.

One day Fran and Fred
went out of the back door.

Let's go out
to play!

To their surprise they found ...

a beautiful big flower!

WOW!

Acclaim for this book

'The short narrative explains the patience needed to grow things –
a difficult concept for children – while the glorious
illustrations celebrate the natural world.' *Junior*